This book is given with love to...

_____

_____

Written by: Heather Lean

Illustrated by: Olena Vecchia Pittura and Nino Aptsiauri

Edited by: Sheri Wall, Glenys Nellist, and
Karen Austin (developmental editor)

For all inquiries, please contact us at:
info@puppysmiles.org

To see more of our books, visit us at:
www.PuppyDogsAndIceCream.com

Sweet Dreams
&
Moonbeams

For Shay, your imagination and
ability to find magic everywhere
greatly inspire me. Thank you
for showing me the way.

Love, Mom

Mommy gives kisses and hugs us good night.

We then close our eyes and magic takes flight...

Pink candy clouds are the sweetest of all,
so fluffy and soft to dance or play ball.

Mimicking penguins, we glide on our tummy,
down icy pathways of snow cones, so yummy!

We wake up big bears from their cozy napping,

and share gooey honey, with tongues loudly lapping.

The bunnies hop as picked petals drift by.

We reach up and touch the lollipop sky.

Capturing stars, that twinkle so bright,
we swing in the sky by heaven's moonlight.

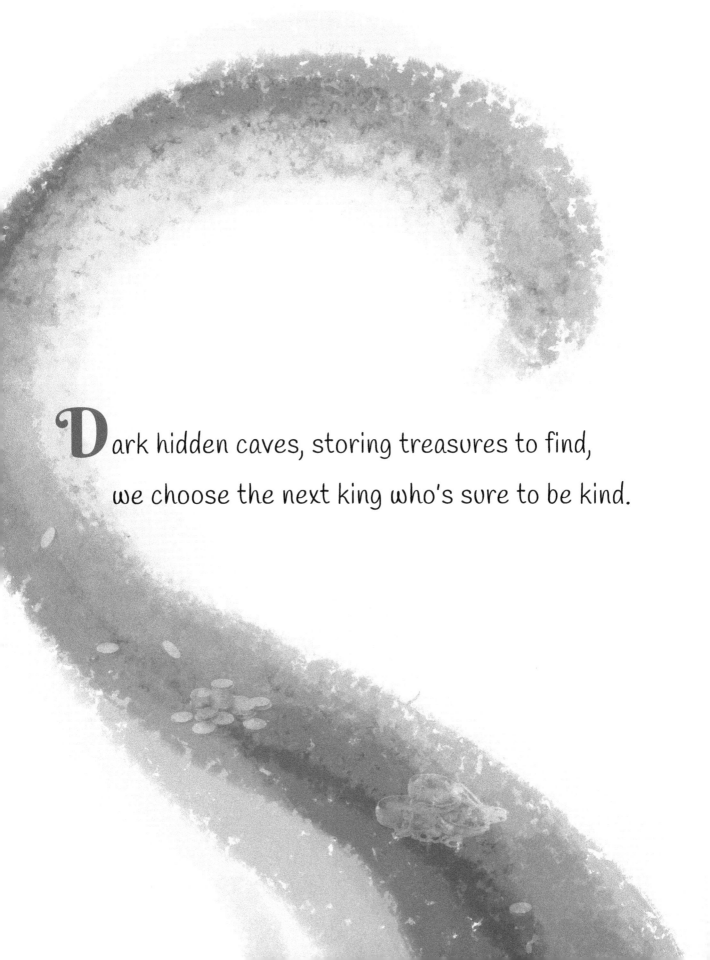

Dark hidden caves, storing treasures to find,
we choose the next king who's sure to be kind.

Riding wild horses, we both take the reins,

to gallop through mountains and green grassy plains.

Dolphins embrace us, from out of the blue,

to give dainty kisses and ocean rides too.

A castle of wishes floats on the ice.

As glimmers surround a true paradise.

Dream of Magic

Up, up, and away, floating high in the air,
sprinkling whimsy to friends everywhere.

Charting adventures across chocolate seas,
with wind in our sails, blowing wild and free.

Waffle cone fountains let all flavors flow.

Ice cream before dinner, as anything goes!

Teatime with critters and pastries sublime.

Squirrels are so friendly, and all speak in rhyme.

We sit by the campfire in candy cane huts,

and carefully roast honey-covered peanuts.

Dancing flamingos, synchronized pirouettes,
make this performance our very best yet.

We take our seats at the seaside café,

where merry mermaids invite us to play.

Mom peeks through the door, what does she see?

Our gentle, soft smiles so heartfelt and free.

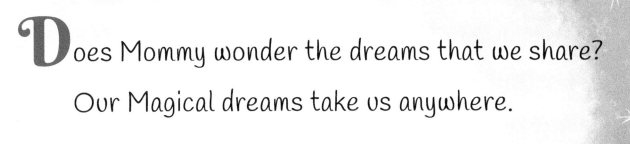

Does Mommy wonder the dreams that we share?
Our Magical dreams take us anywhere.

So, please dream of wonder and reach for the stars.
Believe in YOUR magic and how special YOU are!

 Claim Your FREE Gift!

Visit ➤ **PDICBooks.com/Gift**

Thank you for purchasing

Sweet Dreams & Moonbeams

and welcome to the Puppy Dogs & Ice Cream family.

We're certain you're going to love the little gift
we've prepared for you at the website above.

CPSIA information can be obtained
at www.ICGtesting.com
Printed in the USA
BVHW022228030422
633260BV00016BA/129